Choose Your Own Attitude
Anxious?

Gail Hayes, M.A.

Illustrated by Helen Flook

www.FlowerpotPress.com
PAB-0810-0354
ISBN: 978-1-4867-2701-8
Made in China. Fabriqué en Chine.

We all have anxiety from time to time and that is normal. We also have different thoughts about what to do when we feel anxious. Sometimes we have two different thoughts about what to do. These choices can be represented in two different ways. You can call them Bubble and Slug.

Read on to see how some kids just like you deal with everyday scenarios and learn what happens when they choose which thoughts to embrace: Bubble Thinking or Slug Thinking. As you read, you will choose how each kid should handle each situation. Should they listen to Bubble or should they listen to Slug?

Hi! I'm Bubble!

Hi! I'm Slug!

So Many Things

Oliver had so many things on his mind. He was already anxious about his math test and his soccer game and then he looked at his phone and saw there was a big thunderstorm coming that night.

Oliver couldn't stop thinking about all that could happen to make it worse. As Oliver thought about all of this, Bubble and Slug shared how they thought he should handle it...

Did Oliver listen to Bubble? Turn to page **8**.
Did Oliver listen to Slug? Turn to page **6**.

Slug told Oliver he was right. There are so many things that can go wrong! So Oliver sat with those thoughts all day. He let his anxiety grow and grow until it was all he could think about. Feeling overcome with anxiety, he could barely pay attention during his math test.

At his soccer game, his coach kept shouting, "Ollie, get your head in the game!"

And when he finally got to the end of the day, Oliver tossed and turned in his bed waiting for the storm that was coming. A bad day and a bad night was just what Oliver had expected!

Bubble told Oliver he was right. "There is a lot going on today, and it is okay to feel anxious," said Bubble, "but sometimes talking to someone can help you understand and deal with your anxiety."

Oliver realized there were a lot of people in his life that he could talk to: his teacher, his best friend, his soccer coach, and even his parents. In the end, Oliver decided to talk to the school counselor, and she had a lot of ideas about how to keep his anxiety in check.

With the advice from his counselor, Oliver started to relax. That afternoon his math test went better than expected. Feeling better about the test, Oliver relaxed further and was able to enjoy his soccer game and even play really well.

When he got home, Oliver told his mom about talking to his counselor. "Good decision, Ollie," she said. "It is always best to talk about your anxiety."

Oliver then explained how he was still nervous about the storm coming that night. After some comforting words from his mom, Oliver went to bed feeling amazing. This had been a great day.

Gather in Groups

It was time to start a group project, and Ava was feeling really anxious. She always felt nervous being in groups because she didn't feel comfortable speaking up. As the teacher and kids were sorting out the groups and what they would work on, Ava started to sink down in her chair. That's when Bubble and Slug both chimed in...

Did Ava listen to Bubble? Turn to page **14**.
Did Ava listen to Slug? Turn to page **12**.

Slug told Ava this was bad. Group projects are hard and she should try to avoid getting in a group. Ava sank lower and lower in her chair and began to sweat. While she watched the other kids get into groups and pick fun topics, it became very clear she was not going to like this day.

Bubble told Ava to breathe and reminded her of the breathing trick her dad had taught her. Ava put both hands on her belly, closed her eyes, and took a big breath. She held it for a count of five and then let it out slowly. She did this again and again.

As Ava let out her third big breath, she began to relax. As she relaxed, she noticed two of her best friends had picked a really fun topic and still needed another person in their group.

Ava jumped up and volunteered to join. Her friends were so excited!
The three of them spent the rest of the day studying and laughing and
learning. Ava was enjoying herself so much she even agreed to help present
their project to the class, and it went great. What a fun day!

Quiet, Please

When Liam's parents started yelling at each other, it always made Liam upset. It was happening more and more these days, and Liam just didn't know what to do. He tried focusing on his homework, but he felt too anxious. He had no idea what the fighting was about or what it would mean. That night as he got into his bed, Bubble and Slug both started whispering in his ear...

Did Liam listen to Bubble? Turn to page **20**.
Did Liam listen to Slug? Turn to page **18**.

"This is terrible," said Slug. "It seems like all they do is fight these days."

Slug told Liam about all the things that could go wrong.

As Slug kept talking, Liam sank into his bed and his anxiety felt more intense. There was nothing for him to do except stay in bed and feel sad.

"This is terrible," said Bubble, "but it is not about you and it will not last forever." Bubble told Liam that when his parents fight it is between them and not about him.

Bubble suggested that Liam try to relax and let them work out their stuff while he worked on his. For that, it helps to get moving.

He couldn't go out for a run (his favorite thing to do when he felt anxious) so he started doing some jumping jacks and some push-ups right there in his room.

The more he did, the more tired his body started to feel but the better his brain started to feel too.

As his brain relaxed, he remembered that his parents love him and had told him that many times. Then Liam started to tune out their conversation and tune into his homework.

It felt good to get his work done, and by the time he finished he noticed his parents were quiet. Liam got into bed feeling like things would be okay.

Time for a Change

Charlotte was feeling really anxious. She had felt this coming since the end of last year. She had felt it even more over the summer. And now that the new school year was starting, it was getting worse.

Charlotte's friend group was re-forming without her. Some of these girls had been her closest friends since preschool, but they had stopped including her in things. It was clear they now liked different things than she did, and they were doing those things without her. The anxiety of losing her friends was eating her up. So Bubble and Slug said...

Did Charlotte listen to Bubble? Turn to page **26**.
Did Charlotte listen to Slug? Turn to page **24**.

"This is going to be the worst school year yet," said Slug. "Imagine having no friends and nobody to talk to. Imagine being the only kid in class that has to eat alone."

"Imagine standing on the sidelines at recess and wondering when it will be over," Slug continued. "This is going to be terrible."

Charlotte did imagine it. She thought about all those terrible things and the more she thought about it, the more anxious and alone she felt. Slug was right. This year was going to be terrible.

"Time for a new adventure," said Bubble. "Let's put pen to paper!" So Charlotte did just that. She started by writing about all the things she had loved about her friends and the fun things they had done together. This made her feel a little bit sad but also a little bit grateful.

Next she wrote about what she loved most about her friends, but also about how things had changed lately. Then she wrote about some of the other kids at her school and some things they had in common. She realized there may be some great new best friends out there to discover!

Over the next couple weeks, Charlotte continued journaling. She found herself drawn to some new friends and began to really enjoy getting to know them. She also managed to stay friendly with her old group. Bubble had been right. This year was going to be a great adventure.

Whether you are reading this book by yourself or you are a parent or friend reading it with someone else, I hope this book helps you see some of the ways you can deal with the things that make you feel anxious. Everyone can have a Bubble and Slug on their shoulder and the one we listen to can have a big impact on our day.

Think about the adventures in this book. How did they make you feel? Read the discussion questions below and try answering each one out loud with a teacher, parent, or friend.

SO MANY THINGS

Did you pick Bubble or Slug? Why?

Were you happy with your decision? Why or why not?

When you read about Oliver's busy day, did it remind you of a time you had a busy day?

Have you ever felt anxious when you had a lot to do?

When Oliver listened to Bubble, he went to talk to his school counselor about his anxiety. Who do you talk to when you are feeling anxious? Does it make you feel better?

How did you feel when Oliver listened to Slug and let his anxiety grow so much that it ruined his day?

What do you do when you start to feel anxious throughout the day?

GATHER IN GROUPS

Did you pick Bubble or Slug? Why?

Were you happy with your decision? Why or why not?

How did you feel when Ava was watching other kids pick their groups?

Have you ever felt anxious about a group project or activity at school?

Bubble encouraged Ava to practice a breathing technique to help her calm down. Have you ever tried taking deep breaths when you feel anxious? Did it help you relax?

How did you feel when Ava listened to Slug and let herself feel lonely and anxious as the class chose groups?

What do you do when you feel anxious at school?

QUIET, PLEASE

Did you pick Bubble or Slug? Why?

Were you happy with your decision? Why or why not?

Have you ever experienced anxiety while you were at home?

Bubble suggested Liam try doing exercises as a form of anxiety relief.
Has moving your body helped you with your anxiety?

Bubble pointed out that Liam's parents fighting wasn't about him and
helped Liam refocus on himself and his homework. Have you ever tried
taking your mind off your anxiety to focus on another task? Did it help you feel better?

Slug made Liam feel worse by making him feel like he was part of the fighting. How did you feel
when Liam felt like there was nothing he could do besides feel sad?

Liam typically enjoys running when he feels anxious. What kind of exercises do you like to do to
help you feel better?

TIME FOR A CHANGE

Did you pick Bubble or Slug? Why?

Were you happy with your decision? Why or why not?

Have you ever grown apart from a friend or a group of friends?
How did it make you feel?

Charlotte found that her friends had developed different interests
and that she was being left out. Have you ever felt left out?

When Charlotte took Bubble's advice, she took the time to write down
all her feelings about her friends. Have you ever tried writing lists to help
sort out your feelings about a problem? Did it help you?

How did you feel when Charlotte listened to Slug and began to imagine how lonely she was
going to be?

How did you feel when Charlotte was able to make new friends and still stay in touch with
her old group?

The Which Ugly Fruit Am I? Chart

I created this emotion chart because I think the Jamaican tangelo is a great example for all of us. The Jamaican tangelo is a delicious fruit—fantastic on the inside but a little out of the ordinary on the outside. This fruit chose to embrace its uniqueness and is now most often referred to as the Ugly Fruit. It had fun embracing its differences and since then has become much more popular. I like to think that much like the Jamaican tangelo, we can all achieve greater success by learning to embrace what makes us unique and celebrate it.

As you read the adventures in this book, use this chart to help you think about which emotion shows how you would feel before and after each situation.

Do you notice a pattern? Try reading this book by skipping the Slug Thinking and picking the Bubble Thinking each time. I think you might like how it makes you feel.

Gail Hayes, M.A.

HAPPY

GRATEFUL

CALM

FRUSTRATED

JEALOUS

ANXIOUS

JOYFUL